# THE GUY SURE LOOKS LIKE PLANT FOOD TO ME



INTERNATIONAL BESTSELLING AUTHOR

## SANTANA KNOX

Editor: Sarah Mesh @ SarahInWanderland

Cover Design: Cat @ TRCDesigns

Art: Bri @ FlashFryed

# CONTENTS

# AUTHOR NOTE

This is a short novella inspired by *The Little Shop Horrors*, it is not a retelling, just a nod to the original classic by Roger Corman–who I graciously thank for keeping this piece of art in the public domain.

Possible warnings: death of parents (historical not on scene), gruesome/gore descriptions, un-aliving, maiming, cooking of a human, descriptions of human soup, vile men.

# 1

# RUNA

It's not often I wake from the sound of sharp teeth turning flesh into ground meat. That's only because I try to keep my intimate affairs to the daytime. Chewie is far too loud for nighttime feedings.

"Chewie!" I whine, throwing my pillow at the oversized Venus flytrap chimera.

She yelps like a dog that got its tail stepped on, but it does nothing to cease the loud crunching of her chewing.

"Please!" My begging is deplorable. "We have to open the shop early for the medium tomorrow." I look over to my clock to see that it's too late; it's already tomorrow.

The early 2000s analog alarm reads two fifteen.

It's today.

Crunch.

Crunch.

"Ugh." I throw my feet into the mattress, frustrated, grabbing my only surviving pillow and wrapping it over my head to dull the sound.

She's getting too large to stay in my room now. I had assumed once Chewie reached maturity she'd stop growing, but it seems that there is no limit to my spell. She just keeps getting bigger.

As a witch, I use my skills to keep my metaphysical shop going and the customers flowing in and out. About four months ago I acquired a Venus flytrap that was crossbred with a tiger lily, but I may have *accidentally* dropped an entire vial of *actual* tiger blood in the growth solution. When Chewie here sprouted a trap with razor sharp teeth I had *no* option but to feed her.

Right?

Well, *I* thought so at least.

Except Chewie is nearly seven feet tall now and requires the same amount of fresh meat as a large jungle cat before she starts meowing like a caged predator waiting to be fed. Because *she can't hunt on her own.*

Okay, ethically I fucked up big time.

I was lonely.

I wanted a friend.

I wanted scary dog privileges in the shape of a plant and I should have probably consulted someone before attempting this spell. And I would have, *if I still had friends.*

At thirty, I've either outlived or successfully written off nearly every person who once took up space in my life. My old friends refused to grow and remained in a permanent cycle of self-hatred toward each other, surviving off of morsels of dopamine disguised as gossip that I could no longer tolerate. My elders and magical mentors became either too old to formulate coherent thoughts or like the rest of my family, are now dead and ashes.

A masculine groan echoes from the corner, forcing my sleepy eyes open.

"Oh shit." I scramble off the bed in a hurry. "Is he still

alive?" I ask knowing well she can't answer, turning on the light before I slide into my cozy slippers to investigate.

Chewie continues to do what she does best.

She masticates.

"Chewbacca." I call her by her full name, tone set to chastise.

The crunching stops.

Like a well-trained beast, she opens what any reasonable person would call a mouth, exposing three rows of razor-sharp teeth on the top as well as the bottom. All I can see are the legs of the polo-wearing country-club ass-bag I found at a local dive bar now lodged deep into the throat of my plant companion.

*Okay, so feeding her a human wasn't part of the plan. It's not my fault Chadrick Dickchad over here wouldn't take no for an answer and followed me for three blocks after I left the bar last night. It's definitely not my fault he tried to get inside the shop and then got aggressive when I pulled out my pepper spray.*

It *might* be my fault that the plant I've made sentient has become *somewhat* protective and decided to start turning some of my less favorable encounters into midnight snacks.

It might also not be the first time something like this has happened.

His legs are chewed to shit, minced meat with some shreds of clothing dangling from the plant's pointed teeth. She doesn't mind the clothes, but she still whines as I examine the situation. She's an overgrown baby. I have to grab the stepstool nearby and move it in front of her so I can get a better view into her planthole.

It's hard to see from this far back, but the other option involves crawling inside fully. It's not a problem, sure it's a challenge avoiding getting cut by one of her many razor-sharp teeth, but the issue itself is that I've already bathed and getting covered in the latex goop Chewie excretes from her mouth is not something I care for.

"Can you lean down a bit, sweet girl? Kinda hard to see from here," I ask because somehow she understands me.

I realized that early on in her growth.

She angles herself so that her opening is directly above my head and her mouth comes ajar, pieces of the man showering down on me like a burst pipe—but instead of rain, it's sloppy Joseph filling. Bloody, chunky, tangled in clothes, sloppy joe.

Hold the barbecue sauce, because I'm barely even sure his name was Joseph.

I go to wipe blood off my face but it's no use, my hands are just as covered and cause me to smear it over my eyes further, making it impossible to see. Pulling my shirt over my head, I use the inner fabric to clean the gunk from my eyelashes. That's when I'm able to peer into the depths of the open mouth on Chewbacca's trap where the Rolex twinkles, still stuck on her digestive glands.

Reaching up onto my tippy toes I can almost grab it. "A little more," I grunt as she practically engulfs me into her opening. I dislodge it with a tug, but somehow the action forces her to heave, and once more I'm covered in the first half of tonight's meal. The quasi-digested half.

I gag, but hold it back, dreading that now I'll be spending the rest of the morning cleaning this mess instead of sleeping.

Just what I need.

"Hope you feel better," I sigh.

At least a *real* dog would be eating his own vomit now.

# 2

# AMERICA

"Williams, everyone is struggling right now." I groan exhaustively before moving the phone from my ear for the incoming barrage of criticism he dishes out so well.

"You are not everybody, America Corsetti." He reminds me in his snobbiest tone. "You are the daughter of the senator, and the future president."

"I kno—"

"No, you don't know anything little girl." My father gets on the line like he's been listening to the call the entire time. He likely has, because he's on the same landline as Williams but from the upstairs phone instead.

My father is probably the only person alive with a landline still in his home, but he refuses to get rid of it, and Truman Corsetti will not hear criticism until the day he's six feet under. Especially not when it comes to the plans he has so carefully strategized to guarantee his future and legacy. Hell, I'm sure the man will leave me a detailed outline of how to conduct myself for the next twenty to thirty years if I'm to receive his inheritance.

I don't want his money. In fact, I'd rather run off into the woods and disappear, but the words themselves would probably send the man into an early grave and if anything, I'd rather keep the asshole alive. Mourning the death of a parent is not for the weak.

I know, I've already done it once.

My mother was taken too soon, she was sick, the doctors couldn't figure it out, and before we all expected, she was gone, and I wasn't even six years old.

That's when Daddy hired Williams to watch over me. An over-glorified nanny slash personal assistant who didn't even like children, only the prospect of political advancement by working for my father—who at the time was governor. He stuck around far too long, exhausting his novelty and becoming a permanent fixture in our home.

I'm twenty-five, far too old to be babysat, so Williams is more like a prison guard than a caretaker these days. He follows my father around like a lost puppy, interjecting himself into my life at the first sign of demand.

"You know what we tell you. And this is what we are telling you, *now*," Williams educates me in his snobbiest tone. "We've allowed you to divert from your father's plan the last six years, let you goof off in that school enough to get your little degrees." He clears his throat with a dry cough when my father doesn't interject. "Enough is enough, it's time for you to play the part needed of you."

"What do—" My father doesn't let me get a word in.

"Meaning, find employment in your field, or I will find you a husband by the time the campaign begins."

"That's in two weeks! That's too soon to apply and interview. Most reputable research centers looking for a botanist will need days to run a background check and look into my credentials, Daddy. It isn't enough time. Not with the way things are, no one is hiring, or looking."

"Looks like a husband was the smarter choice then, too bad you wasted all that time in school," Williams says with a curt tone.

I hear the line click, letting me know my father is no longer listening. "Is this for real?"

I don't know why I bother asking, at the end of the day I know Williams is the one whispering these plans directly into his ear. He is my father's manipulator now, the puppet master, having been too long in this house. Seymour Williams is the son he had always wanted for but never had a chance to get before my mother died.

"Your father doesn't make idle threats, Meri. I told you if you didn't have a plan when you came home from college that we'd have one for you." Williams is sour at the mention of college, recalling the memory of his anger when my father let me go across the country for education.

Far from his insidious reach.

It's been three weeks since I've been home now, scouring the city for job postings and leads, doing my best to evade Williams' constantly looming shadow. It's suffocating, I had forgotten just how badly it felt then, why I so desperately had yearned to escape to a school thousands of miles away.

I know he's hoping for the latter, but I pretend like this is a phone call between two people who tolerate each other. "I'll find something, the city is big, there's dozens of research centers, at least thirty labs, and if all else fails, I'll go to the schools for employment." The assurance is for me, not him.

I'm trying to convince myself. A master's in plant biology wasn't part of my father's plans, but I promised I'd make use of my silly obsession and that a daughter in STEM was sure to look great in a campaign.

Neither of them will give me the time or grace to make

good on that promise. My father wants me on my knees for some man, and Williams is dead set on becoming that man.

The only thing I'm good for, according to him.

He's been in office practically my entire life. My mother married the mayor, but by the time she died he was already the governor. Two terms and he was a shoe-in for the senate, the man practically ran undisputed. Now as his second term comes to an end he'll run for Senator a third time before going for the guaranteed gold—presidency.

"America," Williams cuts in before I get a chance to hang up, "I made you an appointment at the hairdresser. Your father needs your hair fixed before the fundraiser dinner. I'm sending it to your calendar now."

I clench down on my molars to keep from responding in some way that I'll eventually regret. My father doesn't give a damn about my pink hair, but I know that Williams does. My father only gives a damn about a wedding.

*Publicity.*

Marriage is the only thing I can offer in his eyes. My degrees, my accomplishments, none of my accolades mean anything to him. Not when it comes to the future president. Daddy wants me dumb, pretty, and silent for photos, unable to stir up a scandal or outrage while sitting next to a man who will someday give him the perfect grandchild.

Except, I don't give a damn about politics, children or men. I just want to grow plants. I just want to stick my hands in dirt and get to spend my time with the things I love most. I've never had a bad day—not when I got to spend it touching plants.

I pull up the first job opening: lab assistant, minimum wage for five years of experience. What a joke. I think about submitting my resume anyway, my favorite professor once told me to never apply for anything I was overqualified for, this felt like such a case. I don't go through with it, the request for a cover letter forces me to close the browser and instead I pull up social media.

There's a kitschy little witch-shop with a small following on my feed. The page says *The Portal* and when I click, it looks like they're on the west end of town. There's a few dozen photos, black walls, lots of eclectic art, and all types of oddities from taxidermic rats to hand painted portraits of a goat-man. The most recent posts, though, have gone viral.

They're all of the same subject, varying photos and videos with different angles.

All of a plant.

I click on a random one and zoom in. It's a strange looking thing, a Venus flytrap of sorts, but either the image is photo-shopped or it's fake. The plant is freaking huge compared to the black haired, tattooed girl taking the selfie, the trap nearly as big as her head. *One month with Chewie,* the caption reads.

I scroll towards the most recent photo, a few more weeks past the last one. The plant is almost twice its original size, reaching the woman's hip, but its leaves are weepy and wilting. This one's caption reads: *Chewie is sick, We're looking for a plant witch/doctor/person at The Portal.*

I'm not one to believe in the supernatural, but a sign from a witchcraft shop is probably the worst kind to ignore.

And maybe this is just what I need to get my father off my case.

# 3

# RUNA

"No, I'm so sorry to have to do this last minute, I hope you understand." I'm hoping she won't hold it against me, but Mabel is impossible to book less than five months out, and she won't take kindly to me canceling her spot at The Portal.

When mediums, psychics, tarot readers, and other practicing witches come to the shop for a guest spotlight, they schedule months in advance to prepare their schedule and their clientele.

Me canceling on social media's most famous psychic the morning of her spotlight because Chewie's just too sick for me to open today is probably the worst thing that could have happened.

People were going to be lining up just to get to see her in person, let alone the client who had booked her.

*And she traveled for this.*

Of course Chewie was the reason she came at all, she's the reason *anyone* has been bothering to come by the shop, the reason I've had any sales at all in the last four months. This plant has been the only thing keeping me from going out of business, but now with her size, I just can't keep her out front anymore.

The community will get skeptical, suspicious, and a man-eating, blood vomiting plant is bound to raise some red flags. The last thing I need is for a SWAT team to come crashing through my ceiling while men in suits try to steal my plant for laboratory testing.

Mabel chuckles, "Of course I understand, Runa, darling. I'm not one to stop a fated encounter. Just be sure to send my cancellation fee by the end of the week, and we can reschedule at your convenience. My clients will understand."

My stomach drops. *Her cancellation fee.* I don't have the strength in me to even ask what she means about the fated bullshit.

I run to my filing cabinet, hands still stained with blood from cleaning the floors all night from Chewie's stomach bug. Yes. I'm calling a Rolex lodged inside her throat a stomach bug, who can stop me?

Rummaging through my files, I pull out the contracts I sign with guest witches and ... there it is. The same stipulation on both sides. If either party is to cancel with less than seventy-two hours' notice, the person canceling will pay a fee of fifty percent of the bookings missed.

I'm pretty sure I'm the one who added that stipulation. Instead of renting out the room per day or hourly, I take a small percentage of the booking instead. Something I found to be beneficial to both sides, and didn't require the guest witch to cough up a ton of money to reserve the space.

I groan, slumping onto the floor in pitiful desperation. Just what I needed.

"Did you hear me, Runa?" The psychic's voice brings me back to the phone between my shoulder and ear.

"Yes, Mabel. I'll send that over as soon as I can." I hang the phone up before throwing it across the room in anger.

This is going to cost me a fortune.

It's going to take me a million farmer's market booths for the shop to cover this fee. I'm gonna be hocking rose quartz to eighteen-year-old college girls for the next six weeks.

Minimum.

I'm only half-considering dumping out my money offerings from Hecate's altar for Mabel's payment when the little bell hung above the door rings.

*I thought I had switched the sign to closed.*

"Hello?" A cheery voice calls from the entrance.

"We're not open!" I shout back, stumbling over buckets of man goop I'm still cleaning off my bedroom floor.

I don't hear another set of bell chimes to indicate the intruder's leaving, instead I hear footsteps coming closer. Scrambling to move and meet them in the store in an attempt to keep Chewie hidden, I trip over an ankle bone and land flat on my face.

"I said we're closed today!" I scream out frantically just as my bedroom door opens.

I'm on my hands and knees, blood, guts, and chunks all over my extremities, splattered over my face and bedroom walls when my eyes fall to the cutest leather Mary Jane's. Perfect schoolgirl shoes with two silver, heart-shaped buckles on the outside of them and lace-frills socks that run up to her mid-calf.

My gaze is pulled up just from the sight of her legs, the muscles drawing up her knees where the few inches above her flesh is left to my imagination. A pink pleated skirt covers thick thighs and cinches at her waistline where a white, button-up shirt struggles to stay tucked in.

A ponytail matching the color of her skirt cascades down

the front of her shirt over her shoulder, and falls just above her breast with purposeful shiny waves. There's a lustrous gloss to her lips, perfectly full paired with eyelashes so long and dark they don't need mascara. She bats those pretty things in awe, her mouth parted, shock setting in as she takes the room before her.

I'm one hundred percent freaking out about hiding the obvious remnants of a murder scene that I haven't even bothered to say anything aside from "Get out!"

However, the adorable stranger is already inside, and I'm left wondering if I'm going to be forced to feed her to my plant for dessert.

"Holy sh—!" She shouts, ocean-blue eyes clearer than crystals dilating.

"The shop is closed!" I yell again, standing to stop her from coming any further into my space.

I'm breathy, panting, gasping for air as I try to push her through the door back into the storefront but her gaze remains locked on Chewbacca. "What the hell is that?"

"Get out!" I scream, shoving her out of the supply room I've made my bedroom.

"You put the notice up about needing a plant ... doctor ... person ... right?" She's still trying to get past me to get back in the room.

"Your timing couldn't be worse." I'm sweating from every single pore in my body, my skin so damp from perspiration that when I lift my hand off from her arm, there's a leftover imprint of dried blood from the night before.

Her eye stays on it for just a second, before Chewie's burp brings her attention back to the door.

"No way." She whispers. "Did that thing just—"

I don't get a chance to deny it, Chewbacca's next burp is so violent it actually pushes the door open, the pungent smell of rotting carcass hitting us both in the face before it closes again.

"Wicked." She sounds more excited than scared, which I think should be a good thing but instead it puts me on-edge.

Mostly because I'm still covered in evidence.

Sure, not *my* crime, but I don't think the police will be taking into custody a carnivorous plant instead of the person feeding it the overly-pushy college guys.

The girl tries to shove past me again but I block her, "Come back tomorrow, please—"

She groans a frustrated sound, "Did I miss her feeding? Ugh." She slumps to the floor. "How often does it happen? I can come back right before the next one!"

It actually looks like her eyes are tearing up. I'm so confused by our entire interaction that it takes me an extra second to realize that she probably thinks I'm feeding Chewie an animal of some sorts.

I laugh awkwardly, wiping the blood from her arm as best as I can, "I haven't quite figured it out yet, she just kind of lets me know when she's hungry."

"She lets you know?" Her expression is nothing less than a child walking through *Willy Wonka's* factory, and she hasn't really even laid eyes on the plant yet.

I sigh, remembering that above all, Chewie needs help, and the majority of the actual man bits are gone and digested now, so there's a good chance I can get away with this. "She's not quiet," I gesture over to the room.

"America." The girl sticks her hand out for introductions, "I saw your post, for the plant. I was hoping I could maybe try to help?"

"Runa," I take her hand. "I forgot that it was still up, didn't get a single reply."

It's pointless to try to open the door slowly because

America practically breaks her way into my bedroom, nearly collapsing on her knees in front of Chewie.

"Where the heck did this thing come from?" She can't control her volume, her excitement is uncontainable.

I shrug, "She just kind of called to me, she was in the middle of a batch of flytraps at the grocery store, practically dead, so they gave me a good discount. I figured I'd try some spells and see what would come of it, and the eclipse was as good a night as any to try."

America snaps her head back to me, "That total eclipse four months ago?"

Guilt floods through me like fire in my veins when I first think of that night, how much she cried and roared from pain at her teeth growing and puncturing through her plant flesh. She was insatiable, with an appetite that grew daily, making it so that no amount of worms or flies were enough to fill her.

Her size tripled within a week, and she graduated from insects to small scurrying rodents around the shop. When I started to work harder than an outdoor cat, I improvised.

I had to hunt elsewhere, provide fresher kill for Chewie.

You can give a woman a fish, and she will feed her plant for a day, but if you put a bar next to her house where drunk men are guaranteed to, without a doubt, continuously prove to pose a threat to her safety ... well, she will feed her plant for a lifetime.

And from their meat and bones Chewie grew and continues to grow. Now four months in, I fear it may be too late. I know there's a soul in there and all I can do is help sustain her.

I think America sees it too.

Her voice is filled with an incredulous type of amazement. "She's ... she's sentient?"

It would be impossible for anyone observant enough to miss it.

Chewbacca purrs into her hand, a different version of the plant coming out than the vicious, blood-thirsty, bitch who has been feeding on Wall Street jerky just a few hours prior.

Her tongue flops out, sticky plant goop that resembles saliva coating America's hand.

"Chewie!" I chastise. "She's not usually like this," I try to explain, but the girl only laughs.

"Chewie?"

"Short for Chewbacca," And just as I say it, my good girl gives out her best impression of the beast, the gurgling noises coming from a place no one but Baphomet himself may know about.

America's laugh is even louder now, full of amazement and warmth. It makes the room feel like summer, it makes my chest hot and the feeling runs all the way down my spine to—

"She's incredible," she breathes out.

I chuckle, my eyes glued to where America's collarbone meets her shoulder, watching the way it moves just slightly with each of her exhales. "She is."

# 4

# AMERICA

I've never seen anything like it in my life.

Her?

It seems the plant is more than just alive, it's sentient, it's feeling, it's not just foliage and plant cells photosynthesizing. I can sense something more in there, in the depths of who she is. She even purrs, like a happy kitten nuzzling into the palm of my hand.

It feels just as good too, shoots the same kind of chemicals into my brain that trick me into believing this is enough for happiness.

And it truly might be.

I don't ever want to be away from this plant. I love all of them, I have ever since I was a little girl, studying them under toy microscopes, picking flowers to turn into potions and perfumes and eventually, I grew up, and I knew I wanted to really understand them.

A degree was a waste of my time according to Williams and my father. Especially useless when it just furthers an interest that will only serve to annoy whatever future spouse my dad will someday choose for me. It's as exhaustive to think about as it is to get through the sentence alone.

"She's incredible," I try to say, but I'm too dumbfounded to be sure if the words even make their way out of my mouth.

"She is," The witchy woman chuckles, her arms crossing over her chest now that she's given up on trying to expel me from the room.

She's absolutely breathtaking, but this time it isn't that plant that's caught my attention. Raven hair down to her low back and bright green eyes that see right through me. It's nearly uncomfortable how deep her gaze burrows into my soul, just from a passing glance. She's wearing a simple tunic, from her elbows all the way to her knees covered in black fabric, and for shoes she sports Beetlejuice Sandworm house slippers.

There's blood all over her, splattered on her face, smeared over her clothes, her entire arm covered in the dried stuff all the way up to her elbow as if she just recently had been in a drive-by fisting. That's when I finally look at the entire room surrounding us; it's messy as hell, eclectic, with crystals and tapestries slung all around the place. Aside from the blood and chunks of flesh everywhere and the giant Venus flytrap *thing*, there isn't much out of the ordinary here for a metaphysical shop.

"I saw your post looking for a plant ... person ... witch ... doctor?" There's only uncertainty from my mouth, no confidence in any of the words I'm muttering. "She's sick?"

"I think so, she keeps throwing up what I feed her, but she's still crying like she's hungry." Her voice cracks, the concern breaking through the facade she wears for composure.

"You really care about her." It seems like a silly thing to be pointing out, but to most people a plant is just a piece of furniture with extra responsibilities.

She nods sadly, "It started about a week or two ago." Runa gets down on her knees, resting her head against the plant.

Chewbacca rumbles like an old engine.

It's the best feeling in the world, the way she vibrates, her energy filling the entire room. It's only spoiled by the graveness of the situation.

"She isn't keeping food down but she cries of hunger all day and night. I don't know what to do." Fat drops of wetness splatter onto the floor just beneath her.

"Don't cry," I whisper, taking my free hand and wiping the trail from her cheek.

I don't know why I do it, my arm just moves on its own, but once it's happened it's too late to take back. "Um, I'm sorry."

The witch is slow to look up at me, her reaction impossible to read.

Chewie vibrates under both of our touches.

"Did you feel that?" She asks.

"Is it not normal for her?" I laugh, pulling my hand back.

The plant bares her sharp teeth at me, something like a snarl showing itself if any way possible. It only goes away when I touch her again.

"Aren't you the plant specialist?" The witch asks me.

I scratch the back of my head awkwardly, "This isn't really a plant."

Chewie growls, the sound making Runa cackle, the joy utterly contagious as it bounces against the walls. "Better not tell *her* that. She's quite unaware."

Runa wipes the remnants of tears from her face with the back of her arm, but the dried blood just rehydrates and smears over her face. It makes her look adorable, though slightly disgusting.

I take a closer peek at the flytrap, examining to see if

anything out of the norm makes itself known to me. "Can I look?"

I'm asking Runa, but it's like the plant can understand me, and she comes open for me willingly.

"Good girl." The witch's voice takes a sultry tone, the words shooting down directly into my core, a reaction that compels every hair on my body to come to a stand.

*She's talking to the plant, not you!*

I think I might need to sit down, but then I realize I already am. My brain generates the most basic question it can to try to cover up the major glitch in my programming she just caused. "How many times has she fed?"

She shrugs, "More than a dozen, for sure."

"And this is the same ... mouth as always?"

Runa tilts her head in confusion. "I don't understand the question."

I smile. "I'll take that as a yes. The traps die after a certain amount of feedings, for normal sized plants usually after the fifth or sixth. The traps will turn dark and wilt and they get replaced. For a plant this size ..." I trail off, expecting her to understand where I'm going here.

"So, Chewie's probably just getting ready to replace her trap—mouth—thing?" She grimaces, stumbling through the words trying to get each one but only drawing another growl from the plant.

"Something like that, I think. The throwing up is concerning, if anything she should be refusing meals outright. How do you offer her food?" We're both playing this weird game where we keep inching closer to each other because Chewie won't let us take our hands off for more than a second without snarling.

Runa awkwardly looks around the room and gives me an unsure shrug, "I don't really ever offer, she just kind of lets me know she wants it when it's around."

*That makes no sense.*

I realize I've said the words out loud instead of just thinking them.

"It's hard to explain, her food preferences are ... strange." She gives me another nervous grimace, "At best."

The trap tilts itself up toward the ceiling, opening up slowly. It makes a wheezing-type of sound, and then the air is suddenly filled with pollen-like powder.

It's hard to breathe, hard to see, we're both coughing, swatting to clear the green fog, but it's everywhere. The entire store is engulfed in the plant's spores.

My eyelids feel heavy, "What is that?" I say, but Runa is already on the ground, her lashes fluttering as she struggles to maintain consciousness.

I fall on top of her, muscles sluggish and numb to feeling.

And everything goes black.

5

———

RUNA

Time is hazy.

It feels slower than normal, though no part of my body seems to notice, my heart still drumming faster than ever inside. My muscles are heavy, slow to move and impossible to lift. My lungs struggle, each breath harder to take than the last. It feels as if my chest is being crushed.

I'm slow to open my eyes, each lid almost sticking together, staying shut longer than I want. Cotton candy pink tufts of hair obscure my vision, I can't make out anything except the feel of a body on me.

America groans—no, she moans.

The sound registers between my thighs like a metal fork in a wall socket.

I wrap my arms around her, squeezing tight, her voice igniting something like a protective instinct inside of me.

*What the hell just happened?*

"Did we fall asleep?" She half-mumbles, her face still pressed to my breasts.

"I think Chewie *put us* to sleep," I grit, annoyed at the overgrown foliage.

The girl perks up, her eyes darting wide open once she realizes the compromising position she is in. She crawls backward to get off of me, but she's just as woozy as I am from whatever was in that stuff.

I can barely see straight.

She wipes her hand over the green dust coating the ground, it sticks to her skin but comes off with just a flick of her fingers. "What is it?" I ask her.

America rubs the powder between her thumb and index finger, bringing it to her nose and wrinkling it at the smell. "Pollen, definitely."

I groan, lifting my hand up to my temple to massage the throbbing, "I feel like I'm hungover."

The girl nods, "She's never done this before, then?"

I haven't even finished shaking my head and America's already pulling a little notebook out of her crossbody bag and jotting something down onto it. "I suspect this trap will die in the next few days, she probably won't feed, even if she cries of hunger."

Her voice is sad, like she understands how hard this must be for Chewie.

"I wish there was something we could do to make it easier for her," I whisper, gently grazing the back of my hand along Chewie's leaves.

America's eyes perk up. "Wait a minute!" She practically bounces to a stand, leaving the room in such a frenzy that it leaves Chewbacca wailing.

The sound is painful, I can feel it in my chest, like kindling growing into a burning flame. It pumps through my ventricles, coursing magma through my veins.

"Come back!" I cry, everything too foggy and fuzzy to make any clear sense of what's happening to me.

All I can do is hold Chewie while she shakes, her leaves

trembling while a song of pure agony echoes from her open trap. It's only a minute or two but it feels far too long without her, the plants' discomfort becoming my own, nearly disabling me as it crushes me to the ground.

I writhe, squirming and whimpering, tears streaming down the side of my face as they fall into my ears.

"Holy Hellebore," America gasps at seeing me on the ground. "What happened?" She drops to her knees at my side.

"You left." I groan, "Everything hurts."

"Woah." Her eyes get big, full of fear as she crawls back a few inches from us.

Chewie makes the same pained sound again, this time, America is the one who keels over from the torment. "Ah!" She cries, clutching her chest, "What is that?"

I pull her onto my lap, comforting her in what way I can, her body melting once she's over me. America sobs from a pain too intense. I know only because my own has barely tempered. I lean my back against Chewbacca, shuddering and shivering through the dulling throb.

After a few minutes she finally speaks, her voice soft and weak, "I was locking the shop door."

I squeeze her tighter, grateful that she had thought of it because the entire day has only been one distraction after another for me. "I don't think she wants you to leave." I laugh dryly, coughing through the pain.

"Well why's she punishing you for it too?"

I shrug, "Hurt people hurt people?" I ask.

"I have an idea." America says, "It may help. Might be worth a try?"

"I'll do anything." I'm desperate at this point.

Her breathing begins to slow, return to normal as the pain dissipates and she's able to focus again. "Well, what if she just needs nutrients? Like a fertilizer? To satisfy her cravings until she grows a new trap that can properly consume meals again."

I sit upright, placing a kiss on her cheek, "You're a genius!"

She grabs my wrist before I can leave the room. "I don't think regular fertilizer is going to cut it."

"Well, the store doesn't really sell 'enchanted-by-the-eclipse plant fertilizer' so, I should start somewhere." I'm debating how much I can trust her, but she's the only person giving decent advice around here and if I don't do something, Chewie is going to die. "I think maybe instead of feeding her ... *meat...* maybe I just give her a liquified version?" I simplify as much as I can.

America nods energetically, "That's brilliant! Do you need help?"

I chuckle, "I don't believe that's up to either one of us anymore. I think *she's* calling the shots right now." I bite my lip. "I don't want to call this a hostage situation, but it's safe to say you aren't going anywhere, America."

"Meri, actually. You can call me Meri." She looks back at Chewbacca, a dimple on a single cheek forming from a half-smile. "And you might be right."

Just then a scowl forms over her face, her attention is pulled to her pocket where her phone vibrates. Meri looks at the name glowing on the screen and sighs, "It's my father." Every bit of lightness she brought into the store with her is now gone and replaced with something that stinks of fear, and anxiety.

She turns toward the door, but Chewie's whine stops her from leaving. Meri looks down at the phone in her hand, hesitating before answering. "Hi Daddy."

"Where have you been?" I hear his unnecessarily loud voice coming through.

Meri clears her throat uncomfortably, "I had a job interview."

"Two days ago," He cuts in, "Is your location turned on? I'm coming to collect you."

She stutters, unable to answer, all the color draining from her cheeks.

"America?" He calls for her, but she just stares at me with a vacant expression, "America!"

"T-two days?" She whispers words I know are meant for me.

There is no way.

I take the phone from her hand and disconnect the call but she shakes her head, "It doesn't matter, he has my phone's location. He'll find us."

"Why? You're an adult? Right?" I look down at her phone screen, a family photo with a man that seems vaguely familiar but the date itself confirms it.

Two days passed while we were asleep.

*No—not asleep.* Enchanted, or something.

Your body still functions regularly when you're asleep, and this ... this was like being frozen in time.

"Yeah, I'm twenty-five." America derails my thoughts, her eyes fixed right at Chewie, "That's not the point, and he's going to take her away if he sees her."

I scoff, crossing my arm over my chest, "Your father has no power in my shop."

"You don't understand," she fidgets with her fingers, "My father is Truman Corsetti."

The name rings a bell but I can't quite figure out which one. "And?"

America sighs, "The senator."

My stomach sinks to the pits of Hell.

"Get out." I point to the door, every inch of my body dripping in cold sweat, from fear.

She's right.

If her father sees Chewbacca he'll take her away.

Men like him are the very reason I moved Chewie from the shop storefront to the backroom, hidden from plain sight. Once she got too big I couldn't answer questions anymore, and the attention she brought could only chance negative things for us.

America's eyes well with tears, but she nods, understanding that the situation isn't fair for either of us. She backs away, but just as she turns to the door to leave Chewie shrieks a banshee sound, a shockwave of pain rippling through my blood vessels and knocking us both to our knees.

The agony is perpetual, it feels infinite, like its seeping into my bones, making its home there just from the suggestion of her leaving.

"I-I don't think I'm going anywhere, Runa." Her laugh is dry, there's no humor there, only fear.

So much fear.

"How much time did you say we have?" My brain is already working double trying to figure a way out of this.

She looks down at her phone, her hands shaky from the nerves, "Thirty minutes, maybe forty-five at best."

It's not enough time, but I'll make do. "Help me load Chewie into my truck."

## 6

## AMERICA

"How did we lose two days?" I'm trying not to freak out, but I can see Runa has no idea either.

Moving a seven-foot plant that weighs as much as three golden retrievers is no easy feat, both of us are wheezing on the truck bed, Runa in one sharp motion swings a dusty blanket over the plant to conceal it.

I'm so confused about it all, suddenly so much more disoriented than before, the powder's effects seeming far headier than either of us realized.

"It makes no sense," Her voice drops to a grave tone.

There's a knock so loud at the door of the shop it can be heard all the way from the back parking lot, where we sit.

"No!" Runa's voice is filled with worry, the look in her face is pure desperation.

"It's too soon!"

The knocking morphs into aggressive banging, incessant and impossible to ignore.

There's no reality in which my father actually sees Chewbacca and just ... leaves her be. He'll figure out a way to exploit the situation and turn it into something he can profit from, something he can use to grow more powerful.

"What do we do?" I ask her, "You're a witch, can't you do something … magical?"

"It doesn't work like that." She shakes her head. "Chewie, be a good girl, and *be quiet*," she urges the plant, a firmness in her tone that makes me clench my thighs together again and remind myself the instructions are not for me. "If you make noise, you won't get to see me again, or America, understand?"

Chewie replicates the throaty Wookie sound, her volume soft though, like she can somehow comprehend that she's being hidden.

"Listen," I want to warn her but there's only so much I can do, "My father is a lot so I just want to say—" I don't get a chance to preemptively say my apologies on his behalf.

We are barely three feet inside the shop again, the back-door closed and locked when my father's assistant bursts into Runa's shop. Bursts is a word giving the action far too much power than it deserves. Williams' uses a rock to break the glass panel, sliding his dainty little wrists in through the opening to unlock the door from the inside.

"The Portal is closed today." Runa's tone is stern, border-line unrecognizable in contrast to how tender she is when dealing with Chewbacca or … me.

"Oh." Williams plays dumb, walking in anyway and gesturing to my father inside the metaphysical store. "Then why was the door unlocked?"

"Young lady." My father's voice makes me wince as I brace for the worst. "I could charge you with kidnapping the daughter of a politician!"

Runa stands there, mouth left open from shock at the

accusation, but it takes me even longer to register what he's trying to say. "Daddy I wasn't—"

He raises his hand to silence me, the motion so familiar that my lips seal on command.

I can feel the heat of Runa's stare.

Is it judgment that makes it so uncomfortable?

"I employed your daughter, I didn't kidnap her," Runa says confidently, not shrinking in my father's presence.

There's something about the way she stands up to him that gives me faith that there might just be someone out there who isn't afraid of him. That maybe he won't control my life until his or my last breath.

"She didn't answer her phone." Williams puffs up his chest, like intimidating a woman half his size is some sort of accomplishment.

Runa refuses to give him any sort of reaction, her response lacking inflection, "We fell asleep."

My father's scowl takes over his face, his outrage only growing as her explanation goes on. He sputters out some nonsensical noises, spittle flying through the room, landing on Williams. He's a lanky one, all legs and arms with bright orange hair, his glasses are round with gold rims and he keeps a matching gold silk handkerchief in his suit pocket.

I hate every inch of him.

My father's mindless drone with a hunger only for climbing the power ladder.

"For two days?" Williams inserts himself into my business, peering through the shelves and tables in Runa's store.

She learns immediately that Seymour is *not* my friend.

I clench my jaw, peeling my upper lip up to bare my teeth at him, but he holds his ground, his gaze full of malicious intent, his smirk so sinister.

"Well?" My father asks, looking between the two of us, "Were you working or were you sleeping?"

"Uh-um," I stutter incoherently, my nerves getting the best of me.

Williams takes the opportunity to leave through the front door, seeing that he's done the task of disarming me enough for my father to trample over, as usual.

"Both," Runa's voice drips in annoyance, "We worked, got tired, and slept. I'm not a monster, I let my employees rest. Can you say the same?" Her stare drifts to the door Williams left from.

"Only further proving my point. This is not somewhere I'll allow you to work, not during my campaign. I can see the tabloids now, 'Christian Senator's daughter, working at pagan Satan shop.'" He grabs me by the wrist, his grip tight enough to bruise. "I've already made arrangements with Williams for the wedding, we will plan a date for March."

The words hit like the gong of a bell, disorientingly painful; I feel them vibrate throughout my entire being.

I collapse on the ground, his hold on my arm only adding to my discomfort, my shoulder joint pulling at the socket when he doesn't let go. "No! Dadd—"

"Sir." Runa's hand is on my father's arm, the look on her face terrifyingly calm. "Please don't touch her."

My father's eyebrows furrow, his hold on me only releasing to free his arm. He throws his entire weight into the slap, tossing Runa against the wall. A few framed items fall, glass cracking and breaking over her.

"Daddy!" I cry again, scattering away from him as fast as possible.

I crawl to Runa, but she's barely conscious, in and out, eyes half shut as she mumbles sleepily. My father's shadow looms over us, ready to strike, to cull away the seeds that we'd just planted before they'd even had a chance to grow.

"Sir—" Williams bursts through the shop door again, his eyes wide, his breath ragged as he wheezes, hands clutching his knees for support. "There's something out here."

*No.*

"Okay!" I jump up, "I'll go with you." Defeat is better when it's on your own terms, at least this way I can pretend like I'm the one in control here. "I'll get married to whoever you want, I'll do whatever you want me to do. Let's just go now, please, before she wakes up." The tears come down heavy and fast, I can't stop them nor do I want to.

There's a deep throbbing in my chest, one I can't find the words for. It's grief, it's heartbreak, it's every type of sorrow you can imagine but for something I can't name.

Something that was missed.

Something that never got to be.

Williams buckles me into the backseat with a look to him that says he's won this one, my father's dog, who always fetches and sits on command. His hand strokes my hair without gentleness, the sneer on his face showing his contempt for my hair color still being pink.

I look back at The Portal for one final look. There's a glowing light from a still-lit candle shining through the windows when my father puts the car in drive to head toward the north side of the city. An immense heat burns through me before we make it a block away, I bite my cheeks to contain the screaming, the scorching pain thrumming through my veins the further we get from the shop.

From the plant.

From Runa.

From everything I know that is supposed to be mine.

I clutch my stomach, making myself as small as possible,

quietly grunting and whimpering until the feeling dulls. It doesn't go away, but with every second I suffer, I somehow become a little more used to it. The sensation becomes almost familiar, like second nature, like breathing.

The pain becomes a part of me.

By the time I arrive home, I'm nothing but a shell, a cried-out version of the girl I was just a few days ago. A phoenix is supposed to rise from the ashes, but from the burning fire all I am is smoke. I hope for the wind to take me away, to carry me back to Runa and Chewie, but I know soon it will be these fancy walls that trap me. And just like smoke, I'll stain them with what remains of me.

## 7

## RUNA

I come to on the floor from a wave of pain, it shocks me back to consciousness with just enough time to see Meri's father driving her away. It feels endless, the kind of torturous misery that won't ever temper, can't ever be soothed. I'm forced to push through it, Chewie's loud screeching beckoning me from the dark alley behind the store, where she waits in my truck bed, covered by a raggedy blanket.

Everything hurts, it's as if I've been run over by an eighteen-wheeler but the only thought in my head is how to get America back. It's as if there's a physical crater now, a cavity that can only be filled by her existence.

*A fated encounter.*

That's what Mabel, the psychic said.

So, I pack my bags, emptying every single thing from the bedroom to the shop shelves. From my sneakers to the hairbrushes, from the smoky quartz drawer and the ethically-sourced rabbit pelts all the way down to my pajama pants.

I box it all, one cup of coffee after the next until it's nearly three in the morning and shapes begin to have a smell. There's only a few old posters left on the wall when I'm done, that and the furniture, but I don't need them.

All that matters is moving quickly.

The Senator said something about a wedding, and just the thought alone makes me nauseous. I don't need outside confirmation, I don't need a plant who screams to tell me what I feel, and I didn't need a psychic to warn me ahead of time.

America is my soulmate.

She's the person for me, the one I'm meant for, and nothing in this world will separate us.

So it's time for plan B.

The one I've been holding onto in my back pocket as the bills pile up and the sales go down. There's no shame in admitting defeat, that I can't make ends meet and that The Portal can't survive another fiscal year regardless of how many prosperity spells I do.

It's only when I'm locking up the door for the final time, and slipping the key into the mailbox for the landlord that I realize I have no idea where to go.

*I don't know where America is.*

Aside from knowing her name and that she's the Senator's daughter, I have nothing else. No phone number, or address, no inkling to where he might have taken her.

My hands shake, the fear of wasted effort washes over me like a deluge of disappointment, I was ready to throw it all away, I was ready to explode my life and start all over—for her.

A cold laugh escapes me as I'm hit with the realization that her leaving might have been for the best. Feelings this powerful, this strong—they can't be tamed, too wild, too raw to be anything but destructive, and maybe that's why Meri chose to save the plant instead of fighting for us.

To preserve what she can of what she has.

"You're leaving, then?" A soft voice whispers behind me.

I scream, unprepared for a confrontation in a pitch-black alley at the crack of dawn. Arms wrap around me to comfort, her smell floral and sugary as she pulls me close. "It's me."

I tremble in her hold, tears streaming down my cheeks as I turn to face her. "You came back?"

"He would have taken Chewie if I didn't leave." She shakes her head, "Plus, going home was for the best." She gestures to the duffel bag strapped to her arm. "Now I'm more prepared."

I take a deep inhale to steady myself, my thoughts, my heart before. I dare ask, "Prepared?"

"Yeah," she nods, "So, where are we going?"

"Meri," I whisper, "You're going to give up everything for this? You don't even know where I'm going."

She swallows, "Well. Where are you going then?"

"I have a cabin in the middle of Winchester Forest, my mentor, she left it for me in her will. It isn't much but, it's across the state line and it's practically off the grid so—"

"It's perfect," she interrupts me, taking the bag from my hand, "I'll load this in my car, is there anything else you want me to take?"

I shake my head, still not fully processing the moment, unable to comprehend how she could so easily just let it all go for me. "I-I don't think you understand, Meri. I'm not coming back, this isn't a quick little trip, and I can't ask you to upheave your life, your wedding—"

She silences me with a kiss, one that feels like her entire body is somehow in it. The kind where our lips collide with need, they part so our tongues can meet and dance, and with just that I know everything I'll ever have to know about America.

The rest can come with time.

She will be mine, if I am hers, because we've both been waiting for each other to come along. It's only in that thought that I acknowledge there's no more pain, only us.

"A wedding?" Meri laughs, "There's nothing waiting for me in that world, nothing I want anyway. I want this, I want you, I want Chewie, and whatever other fucking crazy plants you decide to give souls to." She unzips the duffle bag, wads of cash peeking out through the zipper. "I also stole a bunch of money from my dad's safe so we should probably haul ass."

"Won't he come looking for you?" I ask her.

"Not with the campaign so close, there's too many eyes on him and he doesn't need the spectacle or negative attention from a runaway daughter. If anything, this might be my only chance to disappear. He'll probably say I'm doing research in some tropical jungle once I've hid myself away. My existence is more of a burden than my absence, catch my drift?" She explains with a goofy grin that tries to distract from the pain in her eyes.

"Your existence is everything, Meri. Do you understand me?" I pull her closer to me, waiting for her confirmation as I scan her face, taking in every aspect of her features into my memory, and sealing her there forever. "We're each other's now, okay?"

"Okay." She nods, a rogue tear slipping from the corner of her eye before I can catch it.

"Let's go then."

8

# AMERICA

The drive is quiet, I expect to follow Runa in my Mazda, but she ends up hitching my car to the back of her truck instead so I can ride with her and Chewie. I get to sit pressed against her, opting to lift up the middle console and use its seat in the cabin so I can be as close as humanly possible.

I drift off around the third hour of the trip, it's only when she pulls into a gas station to fuel up that I wake, the rising sun coming up behind us in the rearview mirror.

"We're close," Runa tells me, a big smile on her face. "Pick out whatever snacks you want for the next day or so, we'll come back into town once we've cleared out the overgrown nightshades around the property."

"Probably best to keep them," I tell her. "We can learn to coexist with them, it's the intruders who should be wary."

Her smile reaches all the way up to her eyes. "That's what Lessa would say, my mentor," she explains with a sad shrug.

"Seems like she cared about you a lot, to leave it to you." I squeeze her hand before we exit the car together.

"Hmm," Runa hums, staring out into the road.

Picking out road trip snacks is the most normal thing we could be doing right now, even though I know there's likely already a small but quiet search team trying to find me. He'll give up once he realizes I'm too far to chase, and I will gladly stay quiet for the sake of my freedom, but he'll still try and find me at first.

So I pretend for now that snacks are all that matter, realizing how much you can learn about someone just from their taste preferences. Runa loves ranch-flavored sunflower seeds, but she doesn't actually like the seeds themselves, she just likes sucking on the shells and spitting them out. It's adorably gross, but when I think about the environmental impact of her spitting the little seeds out the window as we drive, planting sunflowers on the side of the road like a bird, I almost wonder if this is what love feels like.

I'm sure this must be it.

She squeezes my hand back, like she knows I need the reminder that she's here, to take me out of all the worries in my head.

It's only a forty-minute drive from town until we get to the darkest corner of the state, at least twenty miles from the last known street light. It's been ages since we've passed another car, but Runa shows no sign of being lost, confidently tapping her fingers against the wheel and humming to the song on the radio.

She slows down once we get to a spot where a tree grows tall with no branches, three more pass on our right, identically carved like the previous one before Runa takes a right turn into the forest. There was a path once here, now overgrown by thick grass, bushes, and fallen branches.

"It was my full-time home until she died, it was too painful to come back alone. When I found the space to rent and start The Portal, I started using the storage room as a bedroom. I planned to spend my summers here once upon a time, but the employees I had eventually left for college, new witches never applied, and I had no time for vacations anymore. I thought about living here full time again, but the drive was just too long for a daily commute," she explains, being careful of the turns she takes with my car still towing behind hers.

"What will happen to The Portal now?" I ask, a wave of sadness hitting me, as if I'm feeling Runa's own emotions.

She gives me an awkward shrug. "The landlord will list it again in a few weeks when I don't pay the rent at the end of the month. Life will go on."

I can't hide my frown. "That doesn't feel like the right thing."

"It is." She takes my hand in hers again to reassure me, "I was miserable, burning at both ends and still not coming up with enough to survive, all for the sake of honoring someone else's dream. It wasn't even my own, Lessa wanted it. I don't know what's next for me, but this feels right, with you."

"It does, doesn't it?" I ask, feeling the weight of the statement myself.

The forest begins to clear the deeper we drive into it, a secluded area opening up where a small cottage is covered by overgrown datura vines. "It's perfect," I gasp, realizing that just days ago I had wished for this.

*Did I manifest that?*

"I think I'm a witch too," I say to Runa just as she puts the car in park.

She laughs, and at first I think she's making fun of my outrageous claim.

*I can't believe I just told a real witch that I think I'm a witch too.*

"Of course you are." She breaks her laughter to say, "We all have it in us, some hear the calling, some ignore it, but I truly believe at some point in our lives we all get an invitation from the universe." Runa makes a funny face like she's thinking about what she's just said, "Well, maybe not *all* of us."

I laugh, the idea that Williams or my father would be taking calls from the universe seeming like a punchline on its own.

"Either way," she continues, raking her fingers through my hair as she pulls me in for an embrace, "Like attracts like, witches attract other witches, or something of the sort."

"Or something of the sort." I lift an eyebrow, staring deeply into her eyes.

She bites her lip. "We have so much to do."

I sigh, defeated, but knowing she's right. I at least got a small nap in, she's been packing all night long and then she drove. "Why don't you rest for a little and I'll start?"

She stares unblinking, a suspicious look on her face.

"I'll start with the bathroom so you can take a bath? Where are the cleaning supplies? Let's unload Chewie first and then we can figure out where to plant her after your bath." I'm going a million miles an hour now.

I'm hit with a strong second wind, suddenly reenergized by the need to care for Runa. It surges through me like caffeine in an overwhelming desire to take the weight off her shoulders.

She's barely unloaded three bags from the truck, sluggishly moving through her exhaustion while I've already bleached, dusted, wiped and restocked the entire bathroom.

I'm filling up the tub, sprinkling fresh lavender petals growing from a tree right outside the window into the hot water when she finally gives up. It feels like a small but mighty victory, getting her to relax and let me take over.

The cabin itself is not as bad as she made it seem to be, nothing like in the movies where it's some abandoned dusty shack covered in cobwebs. It just needed a good wipe, some sweeping, and love. We'll keep the windows open for the next day or so to air it out and it should be good as new.

It's perfect and it's going to be home.

With her.

I find clean blankets and towels packed away in a vacuum sealed bag under the bed, a delightful surprise when everything still has the remnants of dryer sheet smell to them.

She's out of the tub by the time I've finished changing the bedding and lit some candles. A breeze blows in from the open window, the fragrance of fresh linen and wildflowers soothes my nervous system like welcome allies, attempting to dull the growing anxiety.

With my phone left behind it feels like I'm in the dark, waiting for a confrontation that may honestly never happen.

*Will he come after me?*

Her hair is still damp when it falls over my shoulders, her body pressing up against me from behind as she nuzzles into my neck. "Hmm," she hums, giving me a squeeze. "This is perfect."

I can't help but agree, it hasn't even been an hour, but just being here, with her … this is freedom.

I'm sure of it.

"Help me unload Chewie from the truck?" Runa's already got gardening gloves on and she's dressed in denim overalls.

I follow her lead, undeniably distracted by how good she looks in them.

"Are we planting her?"

"Yes!" She chirps, swinging open the tailgate. "I think the universe is asking for it, don't you?"

Her smile is brilliant, it's warm and so full of joy and hope that it eases every tightness still remaining in my chest. I'm enamored with the way she sees things as signs and how her interpretation of those very things determine her day-to-day actions.

She's intoxicating to be around.

I don't know if I'll ever get enough.

"I do." I whisper my reply, but she's already on the other side of the truck bed, squatting to grab the edges of the pot.

Scrambling to catch up before she hurts herself by trying to do it alone, I climb the truck and help her. Chewie looks bigger than she did just a few days prior, there's no way she's grown in such a short time, but I don't recall having to tilt my neck up so much to look at her before.

"It's a good thing, probably," I wheeze, stepping down little by little, the struggle on both our faces borderline amusing as we try to lift and move this plant. "If we waited any longer she was just gonna have to stay up there."

Chewbacca makes her gurgling noise, as if protesting my joke to the fullest degree.

Runa laughs, "You're lucky she's not a Wookie or she'd tear your arm off for that one." She comes back to a stand, wiping glistening beads of sweat from her forehead with the back of her arm. "Where do you think?"

I do a full 360-degree spin on my heels, slow, taking my time to scope out the landscape. "I think right here," walking only a few feet toward the Southeast corner of the house, I point to the spot in front of the window, "she'll get tons of full, direct, sunlight, she has space to expand her roots, and we can still see her from our front window."

Runa nods, "Plus her trap can still reach the front door, and if anything, that's a built-in security system on its own."

I laugh harder than I can control, tilting my head back and making a fool of myself. An awkward embarrassment lingers. Runa notices my discomfort with myself, the way my composure stands and I suddenly want to run away, go home, forget I've done any of this.

"Hey," her voice is a low hush, "I like you as is. Don't be anything you're not around me." Her fingers rake against my throat, her hold becoming firm as she grips the back of my neck to force my gaze up to her, "Okay?"

I can't blink, can't look away from her, so I simply rasp out, "Okay."

A slow clapping sound breaks the bubble of intimacy around us, a vile, sinister, laughter that's too familiar for me to not know from deep in my bones. Williams steps out from a covering of trees, that wretched look on his face like he's just won again. "Wow."

I'm suddenly paralyzed, every possible fear coming to fruition just hours into our plan, the proof of what I've been told my entire life presented in front of me; I will never escape my family.

"H-how?" Runa manages to choke out, the look on her face surely identical to mine.

"You think the senator doesn't keep a tracker in his daughter's car?" He looks at us like we're idiots, taking one confident step after another as he gets closer to us.

I'm trying to ask where he came from, for the details, but I only manage one single word before I realize that none of it matters if he's here to take it all away from me. "W-where?"

"Where what?" He frowns, looking back from the way he came. "My car? It's parked on the road, I wanted to make sure you two didn't sneak off and hide when you heard me pull up."

His sneer is more venomous than the baneful vines surrounding us, full of contempt, as if this is somehow so much more personal to him.

"Why do you even care?" I manage to complete a full thought when I feel Runa's hand close around mine, the simple gesture syphons her strength directly into me.

At least, it feels like it.

"At first I thought I'd drag you home by the hair, kicking and screaming while I delivered you to your dad like a present. I daydreamed the entire drive here about how he'd thank me, what he'd offer in exchange for my willingness to still put up with you and this little ..." He looks at Runa for only a split second, "Interruption of our plans."

"I'm not going." I declare, crossing my arms over my chest. "You might as well kill me if you want to take me home, I'm staying."

He laughs, a condescending type that unnerves me to the bone. "Yeah, you can stay here." His eyes haven't managed to look my way once yet, for the most part they've been locked in one direction only.

Chewie's.

The plant whines, like she feels the anxious energy and can't help but be affected by it.

"Then what do you want?" Runa's voice takes a more assertive tone, her fists balling at her side.

"I want the alien you're trying to hide behind you. The same one you were trying to cover up with that blanket the other night." He laughs, "I figured it was drugs or something illegal but ..."

"Alien?" I whisper, confused.

He shakes his head, amusement still clear on his face as he

pulls his phone out. "Now I get to be the guy who brought in an ET. Your dad and I are gonna be getting the highest clearance at Area 51. Hell, maybe I'll bypass him altogether and go directly to the President with this thing."

I'm so disoriented from his dumb conclusion that I don't have the appropriate response, Runa bursts out in a fit of laughter, no longer caring to present as intimidating.

"Alien?" She cackles, "You fucking idiot, that's a plant."

"Nice try." His chuckle is insulting to our intelligence, he approaches confidently, unafraid of either of us. "Now, the question is, do I want to call in the cavalry for transport, or do this quietly?" Williams lifts up the phone like he's gonna take a picture but I lunge, reaching for it and slapping it down to the ground.

Rage burns from his eyes, his features twisting, as the vein on his forehead threatens to explode. He shoves me with a powerful push, my back colliding against the wooden exterior of the cabin.

I scream, pain throbbing through my body, Runa's grunts of struggle the only thing that forces my eyes to stay open and fight. He will not take everything from us. I'm able to come to a stand but just then Runa is pushed onto me. I catch her before she can fall to the ground, but by the time we've recovered Williams is already in front of the plant. I move to stop him but Runa grips my arm, showing me the shattered phone in her hand.

Chewie makes a warning sound that reminds me of a rattlesnake's tail, the minute Williams' lifts to touch a leaf, the trap opens with a hiss. Still, he moves closer, nothing but wonder in his eyes as he reaches for the carnivorous plant. "Where did you come from?" He asks incredulously.

The trap begins to tilt, it shifts from pointing toward the sky until the opening is but inches from Williams' face. He stands there stupefied, frozen from shock and possibly fear as Chewbacca's rumbling grows from a low hum to a full on growl.

We watch in silence, the anticipation is nerve-wracking, but it can only be comparable to watching a child fall into the gorilla enclosure. A moronic, ugly child you don't care about, and a gorilla with teeth bigger than hands who has a hunger for live meat. Runa's grip on me softens, her hand moving down from my wrist, fingers interlacing with mine.

A crow caws in the distance, both our heads whipping in the direction for a single split second. It's then that Williams' scream fills the forest, a blood-curdling sound that loses itself in the trees, but pulls our attention back to him. His hand is gone, Chewie's crunching loud and obnoxious as she works to digest the snack unbothered.

He shrieks, collapsing to the ground and flopping like a fish out of water trying to survive. Blood sprays and spatters, almost obnoxiously, something like a high-budget Quentin Tarantino film, and all I can wonder is if he'll stop screaming before it fully drains out of him.

"She doesn't like men." Runa shakes her head slowly, stepping toward Williams like the warning was held on the tip of her tongue the entire time.

"You fucking bitch!" He wails, swinging his nubby bloody stump as he kicks out with his legs.

But every movement of his becomes weaker the more blood he loses, his strength dwindling down as he reserves it for his one remaining hand to try to contain the bleeding.

It's then that I realize he is dying.

*Because of me.*

I take a deep inhale, wondering if with the exhale will come the feeling of guilt.

But it never happens.

And that's quite alright.

# 9

# RUNA

I step toward the pathetic whimpering man, hoping to at least get some answers before he bleeds out. "Does anyone else know where you are?"

He's incoherent now, a shade of pale I've never seen on a breathing person, his teeth chattering as he trembles on the grass. How he hasn't gone into shock yet is far beyond my own understanding. When he makes no effort to answer, I press his head all the way down to the ground with the bottom of my foot, his strength only enough to shift his gaze up at me.

"P-p-ple—" He sputters an attempt, as if I'm able to help him in some way.

I'm not, but even if I was, I wouldn't.

"Her father." I ask the more important question, "Does he know she's missing? Is he looking for her?"

"N-n-n—" The man's head barely moves from the weight of my foot, but I take it for the answer I need it to be. "Good. Finish him off, Chewie."

His eyes grow twice their size from my command, but instead of devouring, Chewbacca spits the half-eaten hand back onto the dying man.

"See!" I whip around to face Meri, "This is what I'm talking about."

Her expression morphs from one of absolute horror, to amusement, a lightness spreading over her features as a smile breaks through her face. She walks toward Chewie, stepping over Williams as if he was never here at all. "That's because she's not eating out of hunger."

"What do you mean?" I'm too ignorant when it comes to plants to understand, and I don't know enough about raising a pet to follow her line of thought.

"She's been protecting you." Meri raises her hand, softly stroking the exterior of the trap.

Chewie purrs, contented at being finally understood.

"Well, shit," I laugh, "I knew you were my good girl."

"I'm gonna need you to stop saying that now." America's voice drops to a low hush.

"Hmm?" My confusion lasts for only a second, when my gaze is pulled to her lips, where the pillowy pink flesh is tortured under white teeth.

Her chest rises with a sharp inhale, her cheeks turning a bright pink.

"Aww," I chuckle, a grin showing itself without my permission, "Does my other good girl need some praise as well?"

Meri's entire face turns red, her speech fumbles off her tongue, but no words are made. I close the distance between us, pressing my forehead to hers while wrapping my arms around her waist. "You did so good baby," I whisper in her ear, a squeak of a whimper seeping from her closed lips. "I'm so proud of you, my little plant witch."

The last word makes her gasp, her cheeks dimple but only for a second, because she tries her best to force the smile down.

"I don't know who it was who made you feel that you

couldn't smile, or laugh, or be yourself without feeling self-conscious about it, but that ends now, with me. You got it?"

Her response is a breathy little agreement against my ear, "Got it."

Changing the subject is the last thing I want, not when she's so hot and bothered by just my words. I'm desperate to see what other reactions I can elicit from her, but there's too many pressing things that still need our attention. "We need to get rid of your car and his before your father realizes you're gone."

She stares out into the forest, her eyes gloss with tears. "He'll notice Williams' absence first."

I shake my head, wishing there was a way to go back in time and undo the damage her family has done to her self-esteem. "Because he's an idiot. Let's go sink his fancy car in the bottom of a pond half a state over. Maybe you'll feel better."

She finally breaks a smile that feels genuine. "What do we do with him then?"

I shrug, "I don't know, the guy sure looks like plant food to me."

"I'm serious!" She laughs, shoving me playfully.

"Me too, you said she needs nutrients right?" I ask.

"Yes ..." Her eyebrows furrow, a wrinkle forming between them.

"So, let's make fertilizer." My grin is malicious, because when it comes to well-dished vengeance, nothing feels better. "She needs blood, and he's got more than enough."

I was barely fifteen the first time my mentor brought me to this cabin, *a place any witch could escape to*, she called it. It had been in her family for generations, and she, unwilling to continue her bloodline, felt I was the next best thing. Back then I was just a teenager, pushing down the pain of losing my parents in a car accident. I floated around, hoping to avoid social services long enough to stay out of a foster home until I could turn eighteen.

"How did you meet her—your mentor?" Meri asks as I walk her around the back of the property toward the vegetable garden.

The clearing that was once a defined ring around the property now has become overgrown and unkempt from time and lack of human attention. The surrounding forest threatens to take over, saplings growing too close to the garden boxes. Their roots threaten to damage years of hard work, a dismissal of the blistered hands that made this place what it now is.

*Even if it could use a little more of that human attention again.*

"Lessa found me panhandling in front of a candy store, trying to convince any passersby to pay five dollars for a tarot reading." She asked if I was scamming to survive or if I was surviving from scamming, I didn't understand the question then, I'm still not sure I do now.

"She saw the loneliness in my soul that night, that's what she used to say at least. From that day on she became my mentor, teaching me everything she knew, from setting up altars and manifestations all the way to hexes and uncrossings."

Meri says nothing, only waits for the rest. "I was the annoying responsibility she didn't mean to get stuck with. There wasn't a mom-ish bone in Lessa's body, she was more of a big sister-type, you know? But I put the burden of parenthood on her." I take a breath, feeling the pain of her memory resurface like an old tattoo raising up on my skin.

"I'm sure she didn't think you were a burden, she took you in because she wanted to." America's voice is too soft, too caring, too full of kindness for me to do anything but break apart from it. She's stopped walking, but I'm still going. "Hey." Her fingers wrap around my wrist, keeping me from going on. "You had someone who picked you, who chose you and chose to love you, and I think that's really special."

I wipe the tear with the back of my hand before it has a chance to fall. "I'm sure she only meant for it to be temporary, but I couldn't take the hint. She's the one who had the dream for The Portal you know? I tried after she died, but I couldn't even get that right."

"Runa." America's grip on me tightens. "She loved you, I know because she wasn't your blood and she stuck by you. It wasn't out of obligation. Don't spoil the memory of your time together by putting words in a dead person's mouth."

It's the most serious I've seen her yet, but I'm grateful for it. I hear what she's actually saying, and for once, I'm *listening* to the real message.

Lessa was magic herself, she was witchcraft incarnate, she was the divine feminine, she was karma, she was ... my friend.

And she left me her home, to become mine.

Now ours.

"Holy shit." Meri's shock breaks me from my sad thoughts.

# AMERICA

"Yeah, it's perfect, right?" Runa asks once she sees my attention is beyond the clearing, directed into the dark of the forest.

"Yes!" I squeal, finally understanding her plan.

Just past the line of trees behind the cottage is another smaller, more hidden clearing. A metal tripod nearly eight feet tall takes up the majority of the space, and from the top of it hangs a chain from a loop. It secures on top of the handle of what seems to be an iron bowl, keeping it hanging about three feet from the air.

No, not a bowl, a cauldron.

Below it is a pile of ashes, indicative of the pyre that once heated it.

"We're gonna cook him into plant food?" I confirm, unable to contain the excitement.

The cauldron is at least five feet in diameter, if we tuck him in like a little baby he'll be snug as a bug inside that thing, and if the fire is going all night, he'll be nothing but liquid in a day or two. "Bones are good too, once we get all the meat off of him we can bake the bones and turn them into powder for even more nutrients."

Runa bats her eyes incredulously. "I-I—" she struggles with her words, fumbling so uncomfortably that I'm sure I've crossed the line.

*Powdered bones? Meat falling off the bone? You went way too far.*

"I don't want to say I love you because it's been at best like, a day if you don't count the time we were put to sleep, and," she laughs awkwardly, "the last thing you need is to be trapped in the woods with some crazy clinger girlfriend."

"But?" I bite back the smile at hearing her say she loves me, even if the words before them might have been *I don't want to say.*

No one has ever gotten so close to saying the words.

She clears her throat uncomfortably, "But I know I'm going to, Meri."

Her eyes meet mine for only a second before she shifts them down to the ground again, like she's maybe trying to avoid the possibility of rejection here.

"I'm gonna love you too." It sounds so damn stupid, but it's the only reply I can think of.

A goofy grin breaks through her expression, her eyes moving to where my chest lifts with every breath.

"If we can get him cooking now, then by the time we come back from ditching the car he should be ready to feed to Chewie."

"Perfect."

It takes more effort to get Williams undressed then it does to carry him over to the cauldron in the woods.

It's deep, which is perfect because even at almost six feet tall, we're able to cram him into the space in the fetal position. There's enough pre-cut logs from the last time Runa was here, but still, I pick some dry sticks for kindling. His bloody clothes make for shit firestarter, but we toss it in anyway.

It takes about three trips to the well for water to get enough to fill the cauldron before we can close the lid. The iron is heavy and it takes the both of us to lock it in right.

"Is it going to smell?" I ask her.

Runa shrugs, "This is also my first time boiling man-stew."

Grabbing her hand for comfort, I drop my head to her shoulder and we stand, watching the little flame under the cauldron turn into a full on blaze. It will simmer soon, and then Williams will be gone.

And we will be free.

Runa isn't wrong, and I somehow have a feeling that it's a good indicator for the majority of how our life will be. I'm positively infatuated with her, with the way she makes me feel and the way I'm no longer in a rush to get through each day just because she's around.

We agree to drive three hours past the cabin, in the opposite direction we came from, just in case. If my dad can somehow still access the tracker in the car then he'll search for me in that area.

*If he bothers to look at all.*

We decide not to deal with Williams' car until tomorrow, coming up with a plan to sink it in the same exact lake as mine. This way, a cohesive story can be painted by anyone who goes looking.

It's dark by the time we return home, the six-hour expedition being closer to seven with extra stops for snacks and gas. The ride back is infinitely better. Once my car is at the bottom of the pond, I feel renewed, watching in slow motion as the water takes a version of me that I'll never be forced to be again. It's as if I'm attending my own funeral.

A beautifully welcome death.

Getting to sit next to her in the truck for the second half of the trip is nothing short of agony. Runa's fingers trail the top of my thigh, every so often shifting from a light grazing movement to holding steadily right above my knee. The distraction is borderline criminal on her part, she knows what she's doing, drowning every other thought out of my mind and making every worry insignificant until the only thing coursing through it is her.

For tonight at least.

Tomorrow the worries will build again, not so strongly as today, and maybe even less the day after, until eventually there might not be anything left except peace.

Runa parks the truck in a way that blocks the clearing from being accessed by other vehicles. It feels like overkill, considering how remote this cottage is, but I don't question her extra care.

*She really thinks someone else might come for me.*

It's sweet, but unnecessary. It's done now, it's just me and her.

And Chewbacca.

The plant greets us with a long gargle, snapping her trap upwards toward the sky.

"Is she turning black?" Runa frowns, shining the flashlight to look closer.

"Yes, I told you, that's normal. She'll grow a new trap, maybe even two once this one falls off," I assure her worry.

Runa's eyes grow wide. "Two?"

She practically jumps up and down, patting the plant joyously. "Did you hear that Chewie, girl? Two traps!"

"I said *maybe*," I try to calm her down before she gets her hopes up. "She's still pretty young."

It does the opposite, only doubling her excitement. "So it's *definitely* going to happen then?" She squeals.

I grab her by the waist and bring her into me, tired of dancing around the obstacles thrown in our path today. "Can I have you to myself yet?"

Runa's smirk is seductive, so confident and sultry it just makes me want her more. "Since you're asking so nicely." She tucks a pink strand of hair behind my ear. "We're gonna have to figure out a way to get this color in town. I'm absolutely obsessed with it."

At this point she's messing with me, delaying the inevitable just to see how frustrated she can make me now that I've voiced my physical need for her. "I'll shave it off right now if you don't kiss me."

She throws her head back, letting out a perfectly cinematic witchy cackle. Before I've even taken a full inhale she's already stolen it from my lungs, capturing my mouth in a kiss so full of fire my entire center heats. I feel her hands under my thighs, scooping me and lifting me up. Every inch of my body immediately becomes hot upon contact with her. My legs squeeze her hips, my ankles cross behind her back, and only the thin fabric of my underwear separates her flesh from mine.

I devour her, shaky hands carving along her flesh with a hungry need while my lips make unspoken promises to her mouth. Runa moans, the sound vibrating through my being directly into my core. "I need you, now."

My plea is all the time I can suffer to spend away from her lips, a smile tugging at the corner of hers as she walks us into the bedroom.

Runa drops me to the bed gently before taking a few steps back. She pulls her hair down from the claw clip that's held it in place all day, the long, raven strands tussling softly down to her low back. She gazes down at me, the attention of her stare forcing me to come up to my elbows.

It feels like a thousand spotlights on me, drying my mouth, forcing me to lick my lips while I wait for her to make the next move.

"Take your clothes off." Runa's voice is commanding, but gentle, and she hums appreciatively when I move without any delay.

A crooked smirk paints her face, satisfaction at the way I don't hesitate.

Not when it comes to her.

"You too," I muster out my own shaky command.

My heart races, Runa's movements so slow and deliberate that it feels like thousands of beats pass between her reaching for her shoulder strap and pulling it down.

I want to tear her clothes off. I want to rip them off her body with my own hands and then stare at her until I've memorized every inch of her skin.

Instead, I just watch, biting my cheek and breathing through a pounding in my chest that's so intense it feels like I may faint at any moment.

"Breathe," she reminds me, a soft smile on her face as she drops the last piece of clothing still on her.

There's no point though.

Why breathe when there's no air left in the room? Why breathe when dying right here, right now, would ensure I'd die the happiest I could ever possibly be?

Runa slowly climbs onto the bed, one knee at a time before she crawls over me, forcing me to drop all the way to my back. "Is there anything you don't like?" She asks, her eyes scanning over every part of me.

The question takes me aback because it's not something I've been asked before, not something I've thought about or taken the time to explore with previous partners or myself. "I-I don't really know."

My confession is just as uncertain as I am.

She smiles like she understands, "We'll figure it out together then, just let me know and I'll stop, okay?"

I nod, watching her as she lowers herself closer to me. When her lips touch my breast, I hiss, the soft, pillowy flesh so warm as she parts them slightly through the kiss.

"Ah!" The gasp is involuntary, a feeling building through my spine each time she pulls away and presses her lips to me again.

Her left knee moves to where my thighs split, resting right against the place where my heat builds.

I feel the wet of her tongue when her mouth closes around my nipple, my back arching on command from the ripple of pleasure. Runa's chuckle grows from a quiet to a dark and seductive sound, tantalizing, as if to say everything she does is now on purpose.

There are no mistakes here.

I whine, squirming with each flick of her tongue against the hardened bead, my core tightening as each wave of pleasure rises higher and higher than the next, waiting for the tidal wave to crash down.

"Runa," I whimper her name past my lips, grinding against her leg to feel some sort of relief but only making it worse.

Only yearning for more.

"My greedy girl," she hums a satisfied sound, "I can't wait to feel that pussy gripping my fingers."

The filth out of her mouth only makes me needier for her touch. I squirm, watching her stare down at me like she can't wait to make me come undone.

She doesn't realize I'm already there. I'm standing at the precipice, it would take less than a breeze to push me over. Runa moves her hands exploratively, squeezing my breasts, thumbs tracing my nipples, pinching and torturing as if I'm just a doll in her hands.

I moan, clawing at the sheets, the mess between my legs further spreading over her thighs, dripping down onto the bed. She toys with me, hands rubbing my inner thighs, fingers grazing the outside of my vulva, touches precise and firm and then light and brief.

I'm loud enough to be heard through the trees, her name a raspy chant from my parched lips. She's barely touched me yet I feel like I'm ready to combust, ready to break apart and shatter into a million pieces.

Finally, her thumb presses down onto the swollen nub of my clit. "I want to fill these woods with the sound of you screaming for me."

I cry, biting my lip as I fight to hold back the orgasm forcing its way through.

*It's too soon, I'm not ready to be done.*

I never want her to stop touching me.

I'm not the one in charge, and here on this bed, my body listens only to her. It feels like I'm splintering open, breaking apart from the inside out, convulsing from wave after wave of pleasure crashing over me. She holds my hip with one hand, still tracing my clit with the other in slow circles that prolong my climax.

"Fuck," she groans, "you're so wet and messy, I fucking love it."

I can only whimper my reply, still panting and breathing

hard as I come down. She doesn't give me a chance though, the same fingers now spearing their way inside of me, hooking upwards and hitting the spot that forces my toes to curl.

"Runa," I call her name.

I'm immediately silenced by my own gasps when her mouth makes contact with my inner thigh, those same soft kisses trailing upward. My entire body is on fire, each stroke of her fingers is a shot of gasoline in the flame. When I feel the flat of her wet tongue press on my clit I fully come undone, nails raking against her skin as I cry out in pleasure.

Runa is unrelenting in the way she dishes it out, holding me in place, sucking and licking, her fingers still moving until all of the pulsing stops. It feels unending, and even then, she starts again, slowly, using my arousal as lubricant to insert a third finger.

"I think you can be louder than that," she chuckles. "The crows didn't even fly away."

My eyes widen when she lifts up, wiping the glistening cum from her chin with the back of her arm. I shake my head, "W-wait," I say, stopping her before she can start again.

It's too late though, with her fingers moving in sync inside of me, magma builds at my core. "I want a turn too."

I barely get the chance to say the words before I'm a mess again, mewing and pleading under her to release another orgasm from me. She moves her fingers skillfully, slapping the base of her palm so that with every strike, each nerve screams and the build up feels like it's going to kill me.

I come with my entire body, shaking and seizing as I gush into her hands, the proof of my climax spilling between my legs and onto her face.

Panting between breaths, my embarrassment takes over. "I didn't know I could do that." I try to pull away, but she grips me tighter. "I-I'm so sorry!"

Runa scowls at first, a confused look showing itself for only a split second before it morphs into amusement. "I'm not."

Her chuckle is a seductive low rumble I feel at the base of my spine, it gives me confidence like nothing else imaginable. I lift up to my elbows again, panting hard to catch my breath. "Get off."

She's shocked at the command, moving with uncertainty to the other side of the bed. I pounce, pushing her to her back and lifting her arms over her head. "My turn."

Runa melts in my hold, surrendering fully as I set out to worship at her altar. I release her, though she doesn't move an inch, eyes watching me, unblinking, as I lower myself down.

The first sound breaks through her chest when I exhale just an inch from her slit. The heat of my breath forcing a shudder from her, her knees pulling together to close as she squirms from anticipation. I'm there to stop them though, keeping them apart as I dive between them.

"Shit," Runa curses, her hand coming down to my head, fingers gripping tight on my hair.

I flatten my tongue to her clit, moving side to side before taking it into my mouth. She squeals, pulling my hair and clenching her thighs around my face.

There's no feeling of conquest like it, of hearing her soft sighs and moans, her little sounds of pleasure as I bring her closer and closer to her undoing. She cries, her heels dragging on the bed sheets the faster and harder I work toward her pleasure.

She was wet before I started, aroused from just getting me off, so when I rub my fingers through her slit they glide right in. Every ounce of authority and hardness disintegrates from her in that moment, a high-pitched whining forming at the base of her throat, growing needily with every thrust of my fingers.

"You're so wet, Runa." I'm both in awe and feeling a sense of accomplishment, my own desire for her growing the closer she gets to coming.

She shatters with little effort, gripping and pulling my scalp, grinding against my hand while I fuck her as deep as my fingers can go.

It's in that exact moment when I look down at her on the bed, eyes all wild and hair disheveled, chest heaving hard with her breath, that I realize how easy it is to keep going. How addictive it is to hear her desperation, how all-consuming it can be to want to draw out her pleasure.

I never want to stop.

# RUNA

The sun shines through the curtains so brightly, I forget I spent years begging Lessa to buy me blackout curtains so I could sleep past sunrise. *You're supposed to rise with the sun,* she'd say, already knee deep in work at the crack of dawn.

"How do you like your eggs?" Meri's voice is far too cheerful for this early hour, I groan at the realization that I've somehow wound up attached to another early riser.

*I'll never get those curtains now.*

"Asleep for at least two more hours," I tell her, throwing a pillow in the open door's direction.

She giggles, the sound enough to uplift my entire mood and shift my morning around. Meri stands at the bedroom door, a spatula in hand and a tiny little half apron that only covers the skirt of her dress.

I don't even know where she found the thing; is it hers?

"I wasn't going to wake you, but Chewie's been barking up a storm outside, I don't know how you've slept through that."

The smell of eggs finally hits my nose, the final key to officially ending my sleepy state. My stomach grumbles, the memory of nothing but road trip snacks for the last twenty-four hours hitting me hard as the hunger becomes impossible to ignore.

"I feel like I could eat a bus," I stretch, rolling off the bed.

It's when I open the window to let in some fresh air that I hear my plant crying, a desperate, painful sound that pulls at every single one of my heart strings.

"That's a lot of eggs," I laugh when I look at the buffet displayed on the table.

"I used the whole dozen, I want to go back into town to get real chickens." She gives me a big grin.

"I guess that's one way to create demand," I laugh, in awe at the already set table waiting for me.

Meri's breakfast is delicious, whether I'm just starving or she is a fine cook is to be determined at a later date when my judgment isn't so skewed. Overkill with the sunny side up eggs *and* the omelet, but when there's none left over at the end, I admit I have no place to complain. The girl can have her chickens. The pancakes are fluffy and buttery, crispy at the edges and just the right height. Even the juice tastes fresher than normal, which can't possibly be her doing because she can't control the way the oranges grow.

No—I think this is just how it feels when you're with the right person.

After breakfast we head over to the cauldron, the extra time he spent cooking definitely aiding in the meat falling off the bones. It takes some time, but together we're able to clean all the bones and get them baked and dried enough to crush into powder.

We spend the rest of the afternoon digging a hole for Chewie, our sweet girl cooing gleefully at being able to stretch her roots out and grow without restraint. The pot of Williams' soup goop gets dumped into the hole, nourishing the soil around it before we cover up her roots.

"She looks so happy!" Meri notices immediately, giving Chewbacca a scratch under her trap.

Most of it turned black overnight, the fleshy parts shriveling and wrinkling. If it wasn't for Meri I'd be losing it, riddled with anxiety and sick to death from worry about my plant. She's here though, gripping my hand tight and telling me it's going to be okay.

I believe her.

Once Chewie is settled in the soil, she pulls the bin of freshly baked bones, settling on a femur and tossing it in the blender with a few cups of water.

The greyish liquid is unappealing, but Chewbacca is thrilled the minute it's poured onto the soil.

The trap wiggles down onto the ground like it's trying to nuzzle into the leaves, like a cat circling its bed for the perfect place to loaf.

And then she goes quiet, the quietest she's been in all four months since that eclipse.

"It's going to be okay." Meri whispers, like she knows how badly I need reassurance.

It's going to be okay.

Because we have each other.

# EPILOGUE

## RUNA

It took around six days for the trap to fully wilt and die. Meri held me through my grief despite the fact that Chewie showed no signs of pain or being anything *but* alive and well. After that, it was another three weeks before another trap grew in its place, though just as she promised, it wasn't only one, but two.

I was able to pay my debts off to Mabel with interest thanks to the Senator's money. I sent a little thank you note with it, but I'm sure she already knows everything she needs to know.

America and I spent the spring building her chicken coop so that by the time summer started, all the baby chicks could move from the bathroom tub to outside the cottage.

We were worried at first, unsure if we should keep them far from Chewie or if their presence was going to somehow ignite some sort of dormant hunting instinct in her. They only made her more protective, the traps snapping in warning any time a fox appeared or a hawk so much as landed on a branch too close.

It's been the most comforting part of it all, knowing that

no matter what, she's here to protect us. The first nights were hard, despite Williams being gone, I still struggled with a lot of anxiety, a lot of fears that her father or someone else in his employment would come searching for us.

The feeling lessened daily, little by little, when I'd wake up and yet again, he had not come for us.

"I told you he wouldn't." The I told-you-so tone is only a mask to hide the sadness behind it.

His loss, I'll love her exactly as she deserves and I'll love her enough to make up for what he refused.

When we began to prepare for the next eclipse, there was no question about it, we drove back into town and picked out a few more plants to add to our garden. A decision I'll never regret as I look out of this cabin window and see Chewie happily existing with her plant friends.

The sundews and the butterworts sing in the morning to trick the birds into landing and the pitcher plants taunt the crows flying overhead.

They all have a little taste for blood, but, if you ask me, all the good girls bite.

So remember to *chew*.

# ACKNOWLEDGMENTS

I wrote this story for the theater girls, for the girls who live in my head, and for the girls who live in my world.

BRI

My muse, my friend, my artist–you inspire complete universes to form inside of my mind.

CAT

My sweet little angel, my pillar of support, and cover designer extraordinaire, thank you.

SARAH

Thank you for including me in the original project–The Tenth Muse Anthology will always hold a special place in my heart.

KITTY

We're still singing "downtown" somewhere in the early 2000s–NOTHING I do would be possible without you my friend.

## MY CENTIPEDE

Brynne Weaver and H.D Carlton, your love, your shield, your kindness has been everything I needed in this life, Thank you for being my friends unconditionally.


## ALEXA

My Armor, my sword–I am forever your biggest fan.


## SAMANTHAAAAAA MY BUTTHOLE

And Rose Dioro; thank you for the wonderful work on the audiobook. I am so grateful to be surrounded by incredible women.

To my ARC team, my discord group, my Facebook Heathens; I am so grateful for all of your love and support. You fuel me to keep telling these stories.

# ALSO BY SANTANA

Rink Rash - A Rivals to Lovers Sports Romance

## DARK ROMANCE

Heartless Heathens – A why choose gothic romance

## PITCH BLACK ROMANCE:

No Way Out (DARKLING, BELOVED 1)

No Way Back (DARKLING, BELOVED 2)

## NOVELLAS:

Dreams of truth: A Dark Romantasy novella

## LIT FIC:

Crossed Over: A Novel

# THE AUTHOR

Santana Knox is the pen name of a Brazilian-born best selling author of Dark romance and horror, writing stories that tread the line between sane and sin. An immigrant who has lived a thousand lives, Santana embraces her eclectic collection of life experiences as fuel for her chaotic writing material. A witch, and devoted occultist, she accredits every success to the blood sacrifices and rituals and thanks the Lord of Mordor, Sauron for keeping her soul safe. A mother and long-time advocate for mental health awareness, Santana draws pride from unifying dark elements alongside impactful, heavy emotions and advises that her books should always be taken with a grain of salt, specifically the kind that keeps demons at bay.

Join Santana's Reading group for bonus content, early looks, and sneak previews: Santana Knox's Heathens
    Instagram: @santana.knox